For Mary Usher
P. & E.R.

For John
P.L.

First published 1991 by
Walker Books Ltd, 87 Vauxhall Walk
London SE11 5HJ

This edition published 1998

4 6 8 10 9 7 5 3

Text © 1991 Paul and Emma Rogers
Illustrations © 1991 Priscilla Lamont

Printed in Hong Kong/China

British Library Cataloguing in Publication Data
A catalogue record for this book is
available from the British Library.

ISBN 0-7445-6093-4

FOUR STORIES ABOUT

OUR HOUSE

Emma and Paul Rogers

Illustrated by

Priscilla Lamont

WALKER BOOKS

AND SUBSIDIARIES

LONDON • BOSTON • SYDNEY

1780

Welcome

This is the story of an old old house that
once was new. It begins in the springtime,
in the days before diggers and trucks
and cranes, before concrete blocks
or ready-made window frames.

The quiet of the valley, along the narrow
country track, rings with the stone mason's
hammer, the carpenter's saw and the cries
of the children rolling in the straw.

Week by week, month by month,
the day draws nearer when the family
will move in. Joe, the littlest one,
is the most excited of all.

The house is ready in the autumn.
For luck, Father carries Mother over the
threshold. "Mother! Mother!" says Joe. "I planted
an acorn in the yard! Who'll grow
big first? The oak tree – or me?"

Soon the house becomes
a home. Joe and his sister and
brother know every corner of it –
every nook and cranny.

But Joe has one favourite place. On winter
evenings he curls up in the chimney seat.
My seat, my tree, our home, thinks Joe.
"Welcome," says the house.

1840

Father's Late

Sixty years have come and gone.
Joe has long since grown up. A doctor and his
family live here now. Tonight he's ridden
out on his horse to see a patient, far away.
For these are the days before cars.

In the house Thomas and
Meg wait anxiously. They listen
for the clatter of his horse outside.
"Father's late," they whisper.

The thunder roars. Lightning flashes
across the sky. Out on the road, Father
struggles against the storm. "Get on, Bess,"
says Father. "We'll soon be home."

The wind tears at the oak tree and
rattles the roof tiles. The rain lashes
the windows of the house. "Poor Father,"
sigh the children. "Where can he be?"

The sun wakes Thomas and Meg
in the morning. They run round the
back of the house, picking up windfalls.
"Look!" shouts Meg. "A branch from the
tree is down!" Suddenly they hear hoofs in the
yard. "Father's back!" they call. "Quick,
bring some apples for Bess!"
"As I rode through the storm," says Father,
"I thought of you all, safe at home."
"Wherever you go," says the house,
"I'll be waiting here."

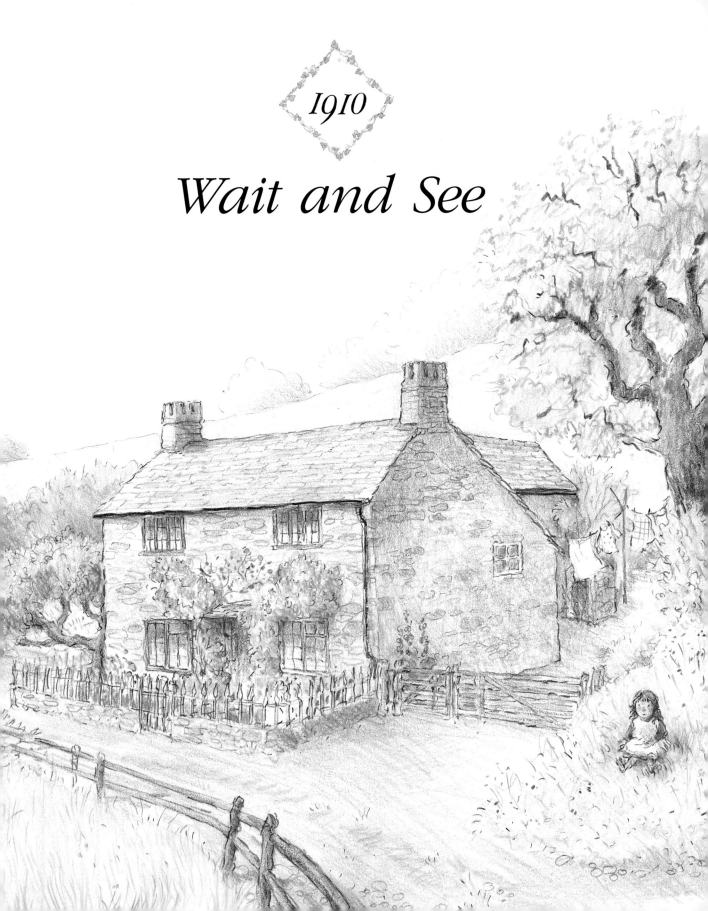

1910

Wait and See

Seventy winters, seventy
summers more. New railings, new slates,
new faces. For one little girl, Sophie,
today is a special day.

Inside the house, there's the smell of new
bread. Out in the yard, freshly-washed
clothes billow on the line. Everyone's busy,
scrubbing and dusting and ironing.

Grandpa has a secret.

He's working in the shed.

"What are you making?" Sophie asks.

"Wait and see!" Grandpa says.

"Happy birthday, Sophie!"
the guests say as they arrive.
"Come and see my new baby brother,"
Sophie says. "He's fast asleep in his crib."

"There's something else new," Father
tells them. "Hot and cold water upstairs!"
And while Father shows off the bathroom,
Grandpa shows Sophie his secret.

A swing for Sophie's birthday!
They hang it from the old oak tree.
"I want to live here all my life," says Sophie.
The house says, "Wait and see."

1990

Where's Henry?

It's eighty years since that day.
Now who plays in the garden? Who lives
in the house now? It's Polly. She's drawing
a picture while Henry, her pet mouse,
plays in his cage.

"Oh no! Henry's escaped,"
Polly wails. "Wherever can he be?"
There are more hiding places in this old
house than anyone would believe.

"What's that noise in the cupboard?" asks Mum.
"Maybe he's hiding inside the piano," says Polly.
"I can hear something up here," says Dad.
"We'll have to take up a floorboard or two."

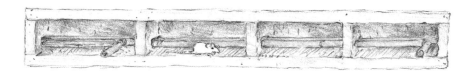

"Hey! Look at this funny doll I found," calls Dad.
"What's this?" says Mum. "It's some kind of saw.
And who do you think this pipe belonged to?
Someone who lived here before?"

Old things! thinks Polly. Nobody
looked in the attic! Henry could be up there.
As she opens the trap door, she hears something
scratching in the corner. "Got him!" Polly says.

That night she draws a new picture and posts it
down the crack behind the chimney seat.
"I wonder who will find it," she whispers.
"Time will tell," says the house.

MORE WALKER PAPERBACKS
For You to Enjoy

THE HIDDEN HOUSE
by Martin Waddell/Angela Barrett

Winner of the W H Smith Illustration Award

The classic tale of three wooden dolls and the changing
fortunes of the house in which they live.

"An atmospheric fable… The mystery in the text is enhanced by fine,
evocative illustrations." *The Independent*

0-7445-1797-4   £4.99

ONCE THERE WERE GIANTS
by Martin Waddell/Penny Dale

The story of a girl's development from infancy to motherhood.
"Deeply satisfying to read and reread … delicately-drawn,
nicely realistic domestic scenes." *The Observer*

0-7445-1791-5   £4.99

A RUINED HOUSE
by Mick Manning

"A treasure hunt, a natural history lesson and a detective story all
rolled into one, which should inspire its readers to regard the outwardly
unpromising features of their own environment with fresh curiosity…
A compulsive read." *Junior Education*

0-7445-4728-8   £4.99